LAURA VACCARO SEEGER

ONE BOY

A NEAL PORTER BOOK   ROARING BROOK PRESS   NEW YORK

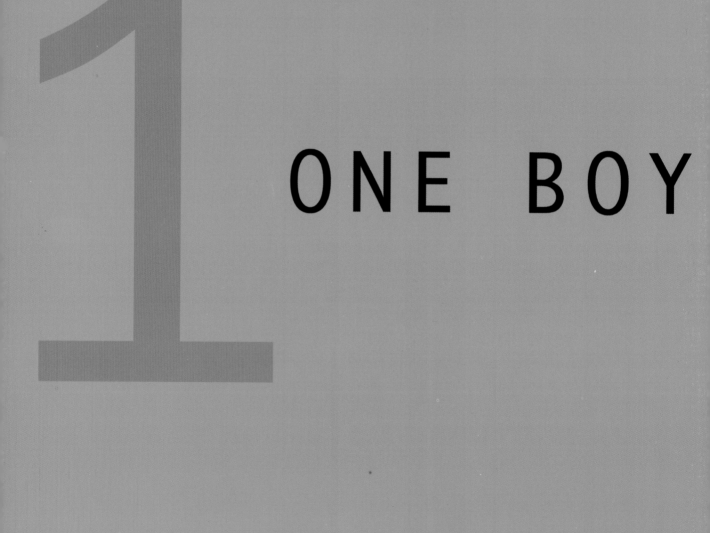

1 ONE BOY

ALL
AL

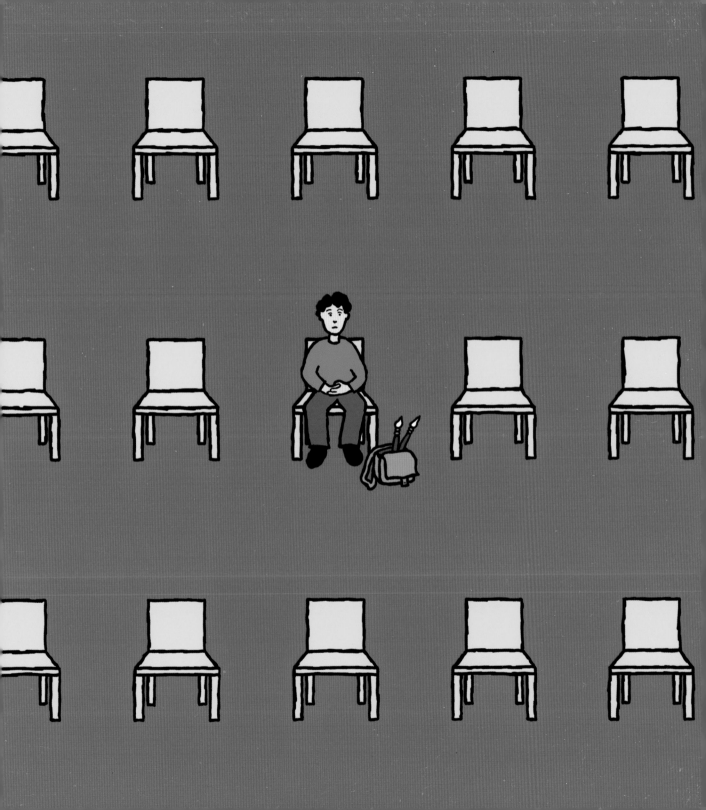

TWO SEALS

2

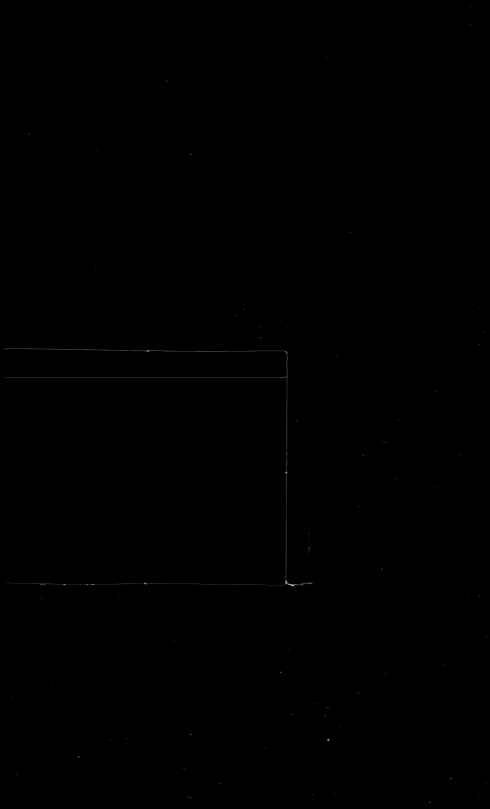

THREE
APES

3

BIG
ESC██ ██

FOUR
MONKEYS

4

HELD
THE ■

SKATE
ON

SIX
CARS

6

ON T

P

SEVEN CANDLES

7

A

CAKE

EIGHT
BROOMS

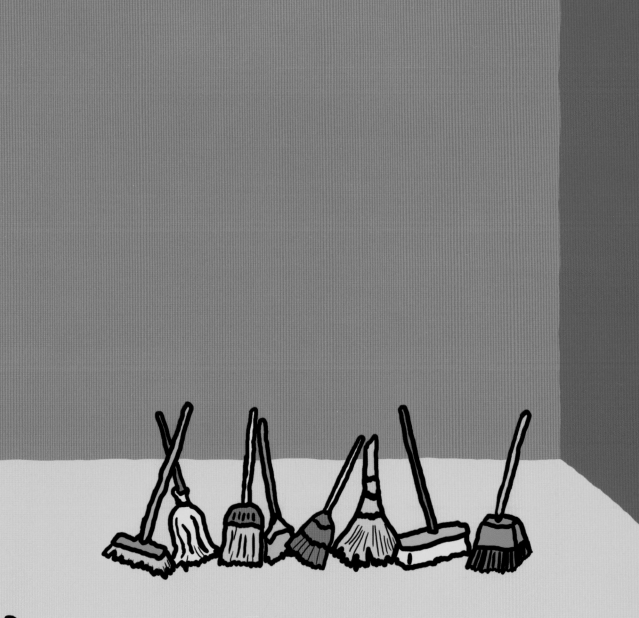

9

NINE
IN
A
ROW

START
TO
G █████

TEN
ANTS

10

IN YOUR

P █████████

ONE BOY . . .

ALL

D█████!

for my sister

Copyright 2008 © by Laura Vaccaro Seeger

A Neal Porter Book

Published by Roaring Brook Press

Roaring Brook Press is a division of Holtzbrinck Publishing Holdings Limited Partnership

175 Fifth Avenue, New York, New York 10010

www.roaringbrookpress.com

Distributed in Canada by H. B. Fenn and Company, Ltd.

Library of Congress Cataloging-in-Publication Data

Seeger, Laura Vaccaro.

One boy / Laura Vaccaro Seeger. — 1st ed.

p. cm.

Summary: A boy creates ten paintings in this counting book that also explores the relationship of words within words.

ISBN-13: 978-1-59643-274-1   ISBN-10: 1-59643-274-8

[1. Vocabulary — Fiction. 2. Painting — Fiction. 3. Counting.] I. Title.

PZ7.S45140n 2008

[E] — dc22

2007045941

Roaring Brook Press books are available for special promotions and premiums.

For details, contact: Director of Special Markets, Holtzbrinck Publishers.

Printed in China

First edition September 2008

2 4 6 8 10 9 7 5 3 1